This book belongs to:

....

....

For Nabila - A. H. Benjamin

For F.E.M and H.E.M - Gill McLean

Editor: Alexandra Koken
Designer: Verity Clark
Managing Editor: Victoria Garrard
Design Manager: Anna Lubecka

First published in the UK in 2013 by QED Publishing
A Quarto Group company, 230 City Road, London EC1V 2TT

www. qed-publishing.co.uk

A catalogue record for this book is available from the British Library.

ISBN 978 1 78171 081 4

Printed in China

The Short-Sighted Giraffe

A. H. Benjamin · Gill McLean

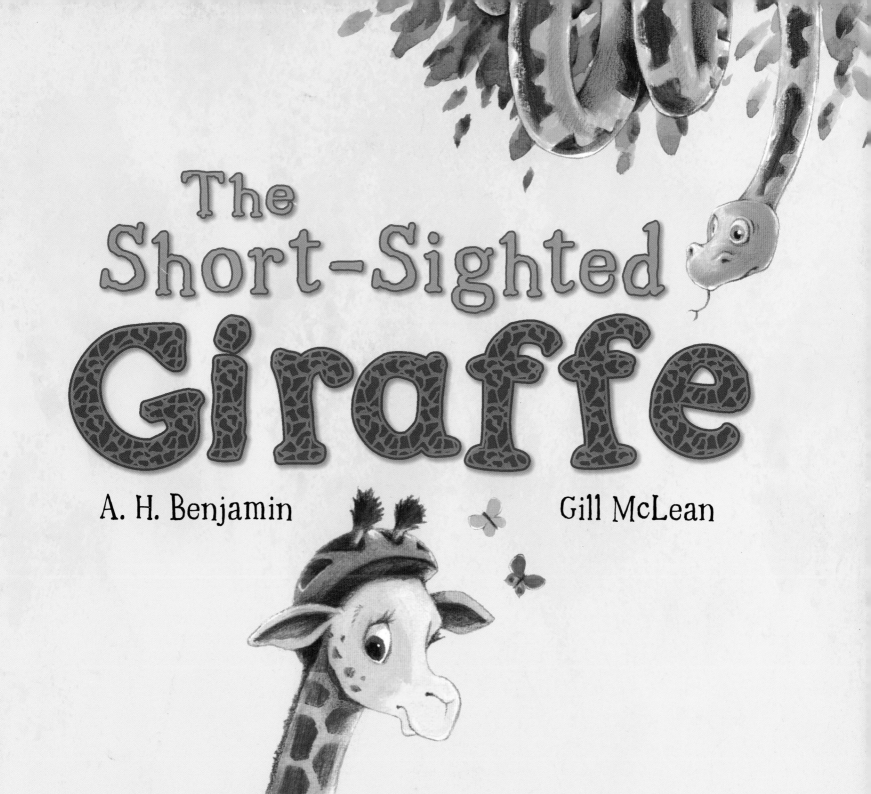

QED Publishing

Giraffe couldn't see very well.

She tripped over Snake and got in a huge tangle.

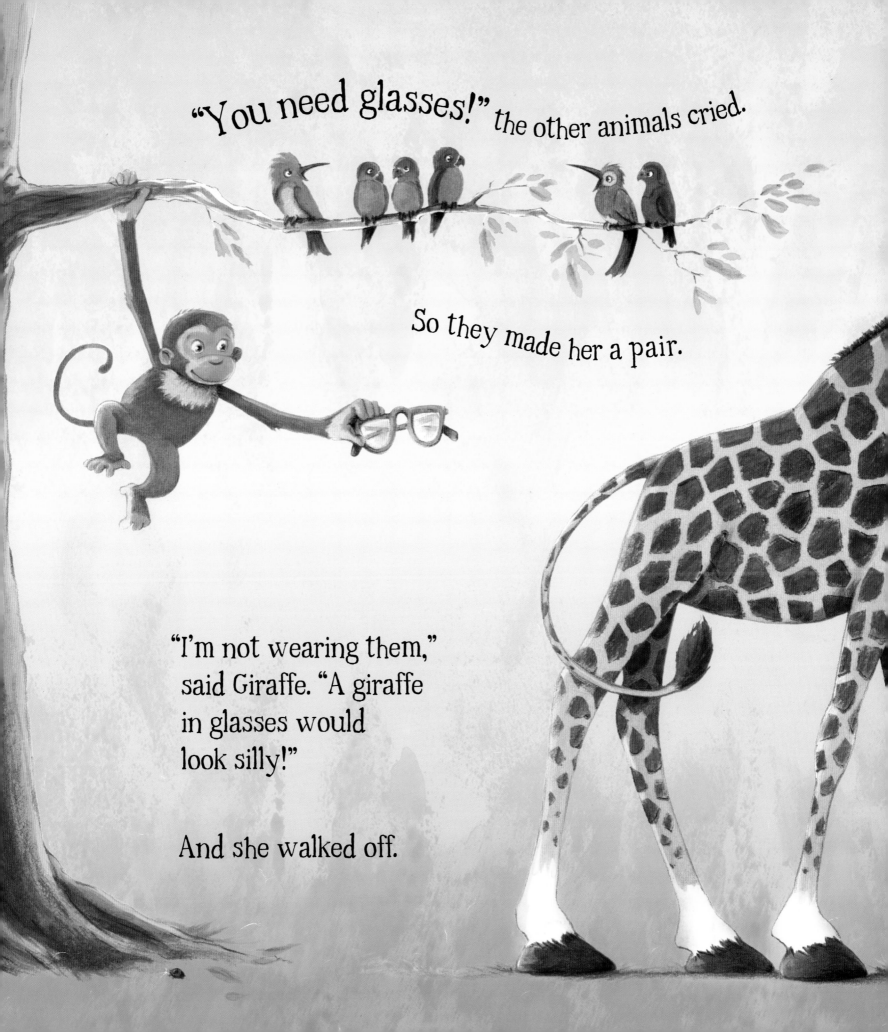

"You need glasses!" the other animals cried.

So they made her a pair.

"I'm not wearing them," said Giraffe. "A giraffe in glasses would look silly!"

And she walked off.

Giraffe would not wear the glasses –
even after she banged her
head on a branch.

"I'll wear a crash
helmet," she said,
"to protect my head."

So from then on, Giraffe wore a crash helmet.

"What's she doing?"
the animals asked each other.

Giraffe would not wear the glasses –

even after she

crashed

into Rhino.

"I'll wear a bell on my tail," she said. "Then everyone will hear me coming."

So Giraffe wore a crash helmet and a bell.

"How silly!" Lion grumbled.

Giraffe would not wear the glasses – even after she hurt her foot on a rock.

"I'll wear boots," she said. "That way my feet will be safe."

So Giraffe wore a crash helmet, a bell and boots.

"She's getting worse," Elephant whispered.

Giraffe would not wear the
glasses - even after she sat
on a thorn bush.

"I'll wear a pillow,"
she said.
"It will protect
my bottom."

So Giraffe wore a crash helmet,
a bell, boots and a pillow.

"How odd!"
everyone said.

Giraffe would not wear
the glasses - even after
she fell into the river.

"I'll wear a rubber ring," she said, "to keep me afloat if I fall in the water."

"She's crazy!" Hippo laughed.

So Giraffe wore a crash helmet, a bell, boots, a pillow and a rubber ring.

Giraffe would not wear the glasses – even after she tumbled into a hole.

"I'll carry a ladder with me," she said. "Then if I fall in a hole, I'll be able to climb out."

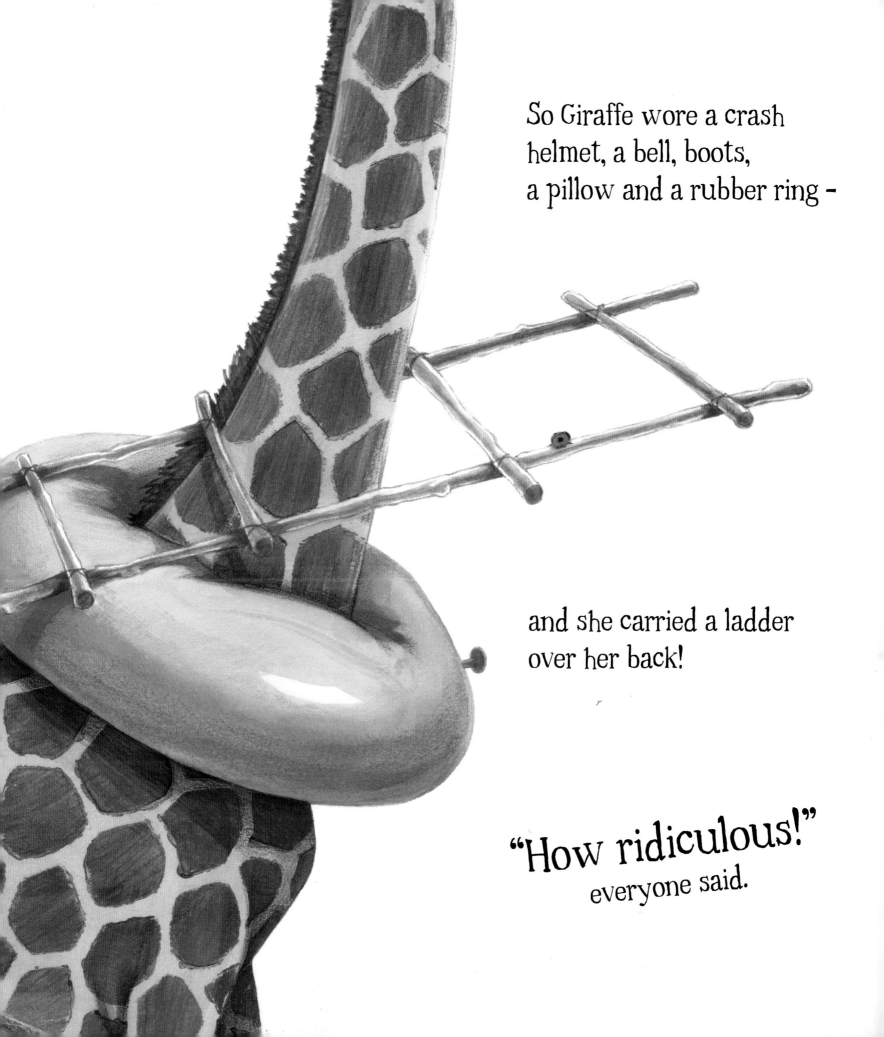

So Giraffe wore a crash
helmet, a bell, boots,
a pillow and a rubber ring –

and she carried a ladder
over her back!

"How ridiculous!"
everyone said.

The other animals
felt sorry for Giraffe.

"If only she could
see herself," Cheetah said.

One night Cheetah had an
idea. He crept up to Giraffe
while she was sleeping and
put the glasses on her…

"Arrgghhh!"
she shrieked, when she saw her reflection in a pool of water.

"Is that me?
I look
RIDICULOUS!"

She took off

the **crash helmet**,

the **bell**,

the **boots**,

the **pillow**,

the **rubber ring**,

and finally the **ladder**.

Giraffe looked back in the pool and noticed the glasses perched on her nose.

"Mmmm," she smiled, pleased. "I look rather smart!"

"Yes, you do!" everyone cheered.

Finally able to see, Giraffe stepped over
a ladybird, and happily strolled off.

Next steps

Show the children the cover again. Could they have guessed what the story is about just from looking at the cover?

Do the children know the term short-sighted? Explain it to them. Do the children wear glasses, or know any children that do? How do they feel about glasses? Did they feel shy or bothered when they started wearing them, or did they feel good in them? Discuss other personal aids such as braces, crutches and hearing aids, and why they are sometimes needed.

Ask the children if they have seen a real giraffe. Perhaps they've seen one in a zoo, or if they're lucky in the wild. Explain to the children that giraffes live in Africa, where many different animals live. Can the children name any?

In the story, Giraffe wouldn't wear the glasses her friends made for her. Even when bad things started happening to her she found excuses not to wear them. Can the children think of other excuses Giraffe might make? What excuses would they make if they didn't want to do something?

Ask the children to draw pictures of different animals wearing glasses. Discuss how the animals look. Do they look stylish, clever, pretty or even funny? What kind of glasses would an elephant wear? Or a leopard? Or a lemur?